THE VAMPIRE HUNTER'S SEDUCTION

KENZIE SKYE

CHAPTER 1

Britney

I affix the black lace mask over my eyes and tie the string at the nape of my neck near my hairline so it doesn't smash my voluminous blond curls against my head.

While most of the other women here are holding their masks up to their faces on decorative sticks, I choose to have mine secured to my head. I need my hands free for vampire hunting. If I come across Henry Banes' sorry ass, I'm going to need both hands to drive a stake straight through his black heart.

Henry Banes. One of the oldest and most powerful vampires in existence.

I hate that I'm impressed by the grandeur of his mansion. Well, mansion is an understatement. His place is more like a castle. When I found out he was hosting a masked ball and that all were welcome, it was just too good of an opportunity to pass up—especially considering how he's my latest assignment from the Department of Paranormal Entities.

I've been working for them for three years now, ever since I turned eighteen and became old enough for them to accept my application.

They contract me to kill vampires. And there's honestly no greater purpose in life for me. You see, vampires killed my parents. I don't know exactly how it happened because I wasn't there to see it. All I saw was the aftermath. A frightened little eight-year-old girl who found her parents with their throats torn out.

I can still feel the scream bubbling up in my throat when I think about it. It was traumatic to say the least.

And I don't know if you're ever really over that kind of trauma, but I certainly found a way to channel mine into a purpose—and that's to rid this planet of every ounce of vampire blood on it.

It's dangerous work, and vampires are wily creatures, but I'm determined and motivated.

I've lost count of how many I've killed ever since I started this mission.

But there's one who's always eluded me. One whose identity I didn't know until a few days ago when the Department finally revealed it to me.

From day one, I've asked the department managers to tell me the name of the vampire who killed my parents so I could have my vengeance. But they wouldn't do it. They said I was too emotionally attached to the case and that it put me at risk. I didn't care if I was at risk, but they've been unyielding.

I've been begging and pleading with no success —until now.

They finally told me the name of the vampire who's responsible for my parents' death.

Henry Banes.

I don't really know much about him. I don't know what he looks like. But I do know through my preliminary research that he's the oldest and most powerful vampire in the city—hell, the world —so breaching the stronghold of his castle would prove nearly impossible.

So, when I stumbled across the announcement for his annual masquerade ball, it was a huge stroke of luck. The universe was handing me this murderous vampire on a silver platter.

I keep my eyes peeled as I make my way through the throng of people.

It may be the twenty-first century, but it looks more like the Victorian era in here. Not only because of the ornate woodwork and Victorian vibe of the castle but also because this is a Victorian-themed masquerade ball. Everyone's tripped out in Victorian wear, the men in waistcoats and breeches and the women in ruffled dresses and corsets.

That's another convention that I chose not to adhere to. While I'm wearing a red Victorian gown overlaid with black lace, I refused to wear a corset and limit my movements in case I end up in a physical brawl with this vampire.

Besides, how do women even breathe in those things? When the lady at the shop was outfitting me with the dress, she laced the stays of the corset so tightly I'm surprised she didn't crack a rib.

She was mortified when I told her I would go sans corset, but I don't care. I'm not here for a Victorian fashion show. I'm here for one purpose and one alone.

My lip curls at just the thought of him. I imagine him as an older vampire with a widow's peak, hard eyes, and a thin mouth like most of the vampires I've eliminated from this earth.

Hollywood likes to romanticize the creatures,

but in my experience, they're just as ugly as their blackened souls.

My eyes flick from person to person, looking for anyone who resembles my intended target. Anyone giving off those skeevy, I-like-to-suck-blood vampire vibes.

"Care to dance, lovely?" a masculine voice says right near my ear. I feel a shiver run up my spine at his closeness. Whoever he is, he's so close I can feel his breath skating across my earlobe.

I turn, ready to decline. I don't need to be distracted from my goal. But my tongue sticks in my throat as I look up into an arresting pair of brown eyes, brown eyes that somehow almost seem to glow golden in the lighting of the ballroom.

My eyes sweep up over a strong, chiseled jawline up to a head of dark hair that's swept stylishly back from his face. I trail my gaze back down over his expensive-looking waistcoat. He's impeccably dressed and looking like a Victorian gentleman of wealth and power.

The man is gorgeous. He's possibly the most gorgeous man I've ever seen in my entire life. I've never had much time for dating or romance. I'm always too busy with my mission of finding the vampire who killed my parents. But even I can appreciate a fine male figure from time to time.

I feel my cheeks flush when I see him staring down at me expectantly and realize that he said something else and that I totally missed what that something was.

"What?" I ask him, my voice coming out breathy.

His lips quirk up into an amused grin that somehow makes him look even more devastatingly handsome.

"I asked you if you wanted to dance. And then what your name is." His voice is as smooth as velvet, and something about it sends a shiver running up my spine.

I glance around us and still don't see the vampire I'm looking for, so I decide what's the harm in sharing one dance with this handsome stranger? Besides, maybe with him sweeping me around the ballroom floor, I'll get a chance to better canvas the area and find my target.

"Sure," I agree.

He smiles a full, even smile, the kind of smile that belongs on magazine covers, as he holds out his hand.

I place my hand in his and immediately feel electricity tingling up my arm from where our skin touches. He keeps his eyes trained on mine as his large hand engulfs my tiny one and he leads me onto the dance floor.

His touch is soft and firm all at the same time. I don't know why it's causing this erratic beating of my heart, but suddenly I'm wishing that I hadn't agreed to dance with him because I know that it's going to distract me from my cause. I won't be able to focus on looking for the vampire when I'm being twirled around the floor in this man's arms—a fact that's made even more blatantly clear whenever I feel his other hand press into the small of my back and pull me closer to him until there's scarcely an inch left between our bodies.

I feel the heat emanating off of his skin, and I look up at him again to see those brown eyes blazing down at me with an expression that makes my breath catch.

No one has ever looked at me this way before. I don't know what it means, but it causes my tummy to flutter like a thousand little butterflies have taken flight in it.

"Your name?" he prompts me again in that voice that sounds richer than the finest chocolate.

He begins to move us around the marbled floor, and I follow his lead with ease. I've never considered myself a good dancer, but he makes it easy, effortlessly floating me across the floor. "Britney," I finally answer him. "And yours?"

He doesn't immediately provide me with his own name. Instead, he repeats mine slowly, his eyes still trained intently on mine. He says my name like he's tasting it, caressing each syllable as he does. Something about the way he says my name while staring into my eyes intently causes a blush to rise to my cheeks.

The knowing grin on his face lets me know that the effect he has on me hasn't gone unnoticed by him.

Oh God, I wish the earth would just open up and swallow me whole. I'm hating myself right now for my pale complexion that always shows even the tiniest blush. I'm not usually one to fluster so easily, but something about this man has me all tied up in knots.

"A beautiful name for a beautiful woman," he goes on, his voice dripping with sensuality.

I suddenly realize that I'm way out of my league here. I might be twenty-one years old, but I'm still very inexperienced when it comes to men. I've only ever been kissed once and that was by a high school boyfriend, and the experience was anything but pleasant. I still shudder when I remember the wet, slobbery sensation of his lips on mine and his tongue trying to invade my mouth.

I kind of wrote off men since then, deciding to stay focused on my goal of getting my revenge. But good Lord, this man is like a god. And something tells me that a kiss from him would be anything but unpleasant. No, this man definitely knows how to kiss a woman. I don't know how I know that, but I just know.

Not used to accepting compliments, I don't really know how to respond, so I shrug and laugh nervously, "It's the dress."

His eyes pin me with their stare as he counters me in that deep, dark voice of his. "It's not the dress," his voice assures me.

My face flushes harder because I don't know if that's a compliment toward my person or an insult to the dress. Does he not like the dress? Now, I'm suddenly self-conscious about the dress, but the saleslady assured me it looked beautiful on me, but then again, she was trying to make a sale.

As if he can read my thoughts, he goes on to assure me, "The dress is stunning, no doubt, but it's the woman within it that makes it shine."

I feel my cheeks growing hot again. I look down, unable to meet his gaze. I'm not even wearing a corset and I feel like I can't breathe. I'm so glad now that I insisted on not wearing one because I'd surely pass out if I was.

My head feels kind of light as he continues to spin me around the room, and when I look up at him again, I realize that he never provided me with his own name.

"Thank you, but it hardly seems fair."

He raises his eyebrow in surprise.

"I told you my name, but you still haven't told me yours," I point out.

Amusement lights his eyes, and I see his lips twitch before he stops and bows as the dance ends. He lifts my hand up to his lips and kisses the back of it.

"Thank you for the dance, Britney, and I'm Henry. Henry Banes. The host of tonight's party."

He shoots me another gorgeous smile, and I stare up at him in horror, my mind racing to catch up to the fact that I just danced with my parents' murderer and enjoyed it.

"Britney?" the concern in his golden brown eyes is the last thing I see as his voice seems to fade away and everything goes black.

Henry

I catch the little angel in my arms as soon as I see that she's fainting. Fainting isn't something that I see women in this century do very much. It was quite popular a few centuries ago, though that was probably due to the overly tight corsets and the women's lack of oxygen.

But as soon as I gather this precious child into my arms, I can immediately tell that she's not wearing one of the blasted contraptions. She doesn't strike me as the sickly sort either. On the contrary, she seems strong and healthy, vibrant and pulsing with life. I can't stop my gaze from honing in on her neck. I can almost see the vein pulsing there. I can definitely feel the throb of her blood gushing throughout her succulent body. I feel my fangs pushing against my gum lines, wanting to descend, but I bite back the urge. Now's not the time or the place.

She's tiny in my arms as I cradle her against my chest and make my way to the library. People part before us to make way, but no one gives us a curious glance thanks to the haze I've cast over the entire ballroom. I didn't want to bring undue attention to me or my curious little angel, so my little hazing charm cloaked us from prying eyes.

Once I get her settled on the settee in the

library, I close and lock the door before I walk back over and squat down next to her.

I reach out a hand and push her silky golden curls back from her face. Her eyelashes are dark and lay prettily—painstakingly perfectly—against her rosy cheeks. Her skin is porcelain, almost as if she's a vampire herself, though I know that's not the case from the delicious scent of living blood emanating from her skin.

My eyes are drawn down to her lips. They're pink and full and lush, like a ripe fruit beckoning me forward. I feel my cock hardening inside my breeches. God, how long has it been since just the sight of a woman's lips was enough to get me hard?

I'm centuries old, so I'm no stranger to carnal pleasures, but it's been many years since a woman has had this kind of effect on me.

I trace my fingertip over her cheek, noting the petal softness of it. The hum from her skin vibrates into mine, making me feel more alive than I've felt in ages.

My eyes are drawn back to hers when I see her lashes slowly flutter open. She blinks and looks around dazedly before those sapphire blue orbs latch onto me and widen. Her breath hitches, and she swallows before she presses deeper into the settee as if she's trying to get away from me.

I frown, less than pleased by her reaction. I'm more than a bit confused by it. Women usually respond to me just the opposite by pressing closer and trying to get nearer to me.

I'm not a cocky bastard. I'm just stating facts. I'm the kind of predator that easily lures my prey in. They can't help but be drawn to me.

So why is this woman—the one woman I want to be drawn to me—recoiling from me as if I'm diseased?

"Where am I?" she asks me warily as she sits up and looks around her.

I sit back on my haunches to give her some space, though every instinct within me is screaming at me to do just the opposite, to crowd her and cover her in my scent, bite her fucking neck and claim her as mine while I thrust my cock deep inside her.

Her breathing quickens as I stare into her luminous blue eyes that are sparkling more vibrantly than the most precious gemstone. My god, she's breathtaking. I'm inexplicably drawn to her. I was from the moment I saw her across the ballroom floor in that red ball gown overlaid with black lace.

But it's like I told her, it's not the damn dress. It's her. It's everything about her. Her essence is calling to me.

Like a moth drawn to the flame, I can't fight the pull to her. I need to touch her, need to know who she is. I need to make her mine.

I've heard the legends of vampires who had fated mates, but I've always chalked that up to mythical superstition. I've never personally known any vampires who had a fated mate, and I've certainly never found one, but I'm starting to wonder if that's what this pull is—if Britney is my fated mate.

But that doesn't really make any sense because every fated mate in history was between two vampires. And Britney is anything but a vampire. I can smell her blood too strongly singing with life. Beautiful, fragrant life.

And while I want nothing more than to make her mine forever, my heart clenches up at the thought of draining her of her life. Would those sapphire blue eyes still sparkle like so in death?

If she is my fated mate, then fate will require me to take her, but how can I keep a human forever? Nature will take its course. She will age and die right before my very eyes, and then my life won't be worth living.

I finally realize she's still staring at me, waiting for me to answer her question.

"You fainted, so I picked you up and brought you here to my library to recover."

She looks about herself again, checking the validity of my statement, her shoulders only relaxing when she sees that she's indeed surrounded by a room full of books.

I watch her hands flutters up to touch the side of her neck. She has an almost relieved expression on her face after she touches the skin there, and my eyes narrow.

Does she know what I am? And if so, how does she know? I've been very discreet about my after-dark activities, and I know I've never seen this pretty little angel before because if I had, I would certainly remember her.

"I've never fainted before," she mumbles.

I cock an eyebrow at her. "Well, I suppose there's a first time for everything."

She merely looks up at me askance.

"Should I flatter myself that it was my good looks and charm that overwhelmed you so?" I try to tease her to bring a smile to her pretty face, but she perplexes me when she just frowns and looks down.

"Something like that," she mumbles again.

My brow furrows, wondering what she could mean. She's a curious one, my little Britney. First, she was blushing and hardly able to meet my gaze, and now, while she still can't hardly look at me, she seems troubled by me for an altogether different reason.

And I don't like these new vibes I'm getting from her. I'm okay with her being flustered if it's because she's attracted to me and young and innocent and unsure of what to do with that attraction, but this is something else altogether.

And I intend to get to the root of it.

She moves to sit up straighter, and I'm at her side in an instant with a hand on the small of her back to assist her.

She stiffens under my touch and pulls away from me.

"Are you okay?" I ask her. "Would you like a drink or something?" It's odd, but when mortals get flustered, sometimes a drink of water or alcohol seems to calm them.

"Sure, just a glass of water if you don't mind," she answers while she nervously twists her fingers in her lap.

I survey her for a moment longer before I turn my back and head over to the drink tray where there's water and an assortment of alcohols and decanters laid out.

I hear just the slightest rustling behind me—so slight that were I not what I am I wouldn't have even heard it. I turn in a flash and watch as Britney's eyes widen at my superhuman speed. She's wielding a wooden stake in her hand and getting ready to plunge it into my back.

I grab her wrist, taking care not to be too rough but applying just enough pressure to cause her to release the stake.

It clatters to the floor between us, and she looks up at me with anger flaring in her eyes. I blink, surprised by the rage I see there. I'd expected a flash of fear after her failed attempt on my life. That's usually what I see when I stop someone from killing me and they realize their mistake.

But not Britney. She's staring up at me bravely, her pretty little chin lifted defiantly and her eyes flashing fire.

I know it's twisted, but something about the angry flush to her cheeks and the fire spitting from her eyes turns me on like nothing ever has before.

The woman just tried to kill me, and yet I've never wanted anyone more.

I smirk and give her a little tug, pulling her to me and closing the distance between us until her body is flush with mine. I band my other arm firmly around her back and revel in the feeling of her little breasts and stomach pressed completely up against me.

I can feel her thighs touching my own, and her head tilts back to stare up at me. She's such a tiny little thing, a fact that's made even starker with her pressed up against my large body this way. I marvel at the size difference between us and the rush of protectiveness and possessiveness that wells up within me.

This poor unwitting little angel that stumbled into my spider's web...

I should be angry that she just tried to kill me, but instead, I'm feeling a thrill of life like I haven't felt in centuries.

"And there it is," I murmur as I continue to gaze down into those blazing sapphire eyes.

If I wasn't certain before that this little human is my mate, I am now. The feeling of her body pressing against mine feels too right. I haven't even tasted her lips—much less her blood—yet, one truth is clear.

Britney is *mine*.

CHAPTER 2

Britney

"Unhand me, you fiend!" I hiss at the vampire who holds me securely in his arms. My face is flaming both in anger and at his nearness. The feeling of his entire body pressed flush up against mine is doing all sorts of crazy and unsettling things to my body. I feel a strange wetness between my legs as well as a pulsing that makes me hyperaware of everything.

He has the audacity to laugh, his chest rumbling and that rumble traveling straight through me. His arrogance only serves to incense me further so that I struggle in his hold, pushing against his chest that's like hard, cold granite.

My efforts are futile, though, for there's no budging him. He's impossibly strong. It was foolish of me to think that I would ever be able to get the upper hand on him.

I now know why Henry is the most dangerous and powerful vampire in the city. It's not just that he's the oldest and that he's incredibly strong, but he's seductively handsome and charming as well. He even had me fooled in the beginning. I didn't have a clue who or what he was until he confessed his name to me.

And that knowledge stings my pride a bit. I've always prided myself on being able to sniff out a vampire, yet this one had held me in his arms, and I had been completely unaware.

"A fiend, you say?" his voice dripping with amusement. "Such strong words for such a little thing." I feel his thumbs rubbing circles on the small of my back and fight the shiver of delight that threatens to run through me. I don't want to admit that his touch feels good.

"Let me go," I hiss at him again, but he just pulls me even closer.

"What if I don't want to let you go, Britney?" His voice is seductively low and husky.

My breath stutters, and I feel my heart beating

erratically in my chest. I scowl at my body's traitorous response to him and renew my effort to get away from him.

"I don't want anything to do with a murderer," I spit at him with all the venom I can muster.

That seems to do the trick because he suddenly releases me as if burned.

He stumbles back from me and frowns. "Murderer? What makes you say that?"

I scoff. He actually looks genuinely shocked and hurt that I accused him of murder, which is laughable at best since he's a bloodsucker.

"That's what your kind does, isn't it?" I cross my arms across my chest as I glare at him.

He doesn't answer. Instead, his frown only deepens before he decides to play dumb. "My kind?" he asks as if he has no idea what I'm referring to.

"Don't play dumb with me," I warn him. "I know exactly who and what you are."

He takes a step toward me, and I fight the instinct to take a step back. I refuse to show fear in the face of this vampire.

"And what, pray tell, little one, is that?" His voice is like liquid chocolate. It warms my skin with its decadence. Low and smooth, he sounds completely unconcerned with the course of our conversation. Of course, he would be, though. Vampires are notoriously cocky. They think they're indestructible, but they're not. I've rid the earth of plenty of them, and Henry is soon to be one more.

When I don't immediately answer him, he hits me with another question. "Why don't you tell me why you tried to stab me in the back just now with a wooden stake, hmm?" He asks the question like he's speaking to a recalcitrant child. He takes another step and completely closes the distance between us, putting a finger to my chin to tilt my head up to meet his golden brown gaze.

"Because you're a vampire." I finally find the voice to answer him, and I try my best to make that voice sound as strong as possible even though the touch of his finger on my chin is burning me like a brand.

He doesn't immediately respond to my accusation. Instead, he grips my chin in his strong hand and tilts my head this way and that as if he's studying a specimen, looking for any sign of imperfection.

My cheeks flush under his strange perusal, and then he tilts my head to the side. He moves his lips down to my neck, and I tense. I feel the brush of his lips and his breath fanning over my tender skin as she rasps lowly. "If I'm a vampire, then by all accounts, I should be biting your neck and sipping from your blood, shouldn't I?"

I hear him inhale deeply as if he's an animal scenting me. I should be struggling to get away from him, but I'm like a willing lamb set before the slaughter. I'm suddenly lax in his hold, and I feel a tingling throb in my neck right where his lips are hovering, almost as if my body wants him to bite me.

I'm transfixed with both this odd want and horror at that desire. Then, I feel his lips press very gently against my neck. He kisses my throbbing flesh tenderly before he finally pulls back and then gazes back down at me.

I gasp when I see that his eyes are glowing fully golden now, no brown in sight anymore.

"I may be a vampire, little one, but I'm no murderer," Henry finally confesses, his jaw clenching strong and proud.

I let out a breathy laugh. Is he deluding himself? He really looks like he believes what he says. "How can you say that when you drink blood to survive?"

His eyes pin me with their intensity. He speaks slowly when he speaks again. "It's true. I drink blood for survival, but drinking blood doesn't always have to end with the draining of life, little one."

I blink up at him, shocked that I never considered that. I always just assumed that all vampires drank until they drained their victims of life. The Department told me as much.

My earlier anger is rekindled when I think of the Department and my parents' death. Henry is a bloodsucker. I can't trust a word he says. The Department confirmed he's the vampire who killed my parents, and by god, I will get my revenge.

I snort and yank myself out of his grasp. I don't fool myself that I was actually strong enough to break the vampire's hold. It was more like I shocked him with my movements, so he released me.

Still, my head is already feeling clearer with the few steps of distance I've put between us. "Even if that is true," I spit at him, "you certainly didn't offer that courtesy to my parents when you ripped their throats out."

Pain claws at me as the memory of my parent's bloodied bodies on the floor grips at my mind.

Henry's brows pull down in confusion, but I'm beyond giving him the benefit of the doubt. He's a monster, and monsters will do and say anything to wreck confusion. He's just trying to trip me up. He's probably having fun toying with me.

Did he do the same with my parents? Did he taunt them before he ripped their lives from them? The thought sends a feral scream clawing up my throat, and before I can think my actions through, I'm launching myself at Henry with no weapon other than my bare hands, nothing but the pain in my heart driving me to near madness.

Henry

My eyes widen when Britney suddenly launches herself at me. She's clawing at me like a little hell-cat, her nails tearing at my clothes and raking at my skin. She draws blood, but my wounds instantly heal themselves. Her eyes go wide and even more feral when she sees that, and a tortured sob that goes straight to my soul breaks forth from her beautiful lips.

She's lashing out at me—wrongly I might add for I know I didn't kill her parents, whoever they were, because of the simple fact that I haven't drained a human of life for at least a century. I finally mastered the art of taking my sustenance without killing my prey, so even if I did feed from her parents, I know I didn't kill them.

But for some reason, Britney thinks I did, and while another vampire might become angry at her irrational attempts on their life, I can't ignore her pain.

So, when another strangled sob escapes her chest and her wide eyes look up at me brimming with the tears of a broken, shattered soul, I can't fight the instinct to comfort her.

I pull her into my arms again, holding her head close to my chest, though this time I'm not holding her to assuage my own lust and desire but to calm her and offer whatever reassurance I can that I understand her pain.

That doesn't mean that I still don't savor the feeling of her tiny form in my arms, though.

As soon as her cheek meets my chest, the damn breaks free, and her entire body is wracked with sobs.

She's suddenly clinging to me, her little hands clutching at my shirt as she buries her face in my chest, her tears soaking through the thin fabric of my shirt to wet my skin with their sweetness.

And god, I truly am a monster for while I want

to comfort her, I also have the overwhelming urge to taste those tears.

I don't speak. I know no empty platitudes will take away her pain. Instead, I merely stroke her hair like I would a frightened kitten while she weeps in my arms.

She cries for so long I can't help wondering if she's ever allowed herself to grieve for her parents before.

I'm also wondering just what happened to them and why she's under the impression I'm the one who did it.

Those are questions I'll get the answers to in due time, though.

Now, this precious angel is taking comfort in *me* of all creatures, and while I realize it might simply be because I'm the nearest breathing thing near her, my chest still swells with pride that I might be able to soothe her somewhat.

The shaking in her shoulders finally starts to subside, and she quiets.

She stays with her head pressed against my chest for a long while after she's quieted. I think she's embarrassed that she lost control and is hesitant to show her face after seeking solace from the very monster she believes murdered her folks.

"I promise you, Britney," I tell her softly, willing her to believe me, "*I* didn't murder your parents."

She sniffs and finally pulls back from me, looking up at me with red-rimmed eyes that are somehow made even more luminous and beautiful with their tear stains. "But how can you possibly know that? You don't even know who they are or what they looked like. How do you know they weren't one of your...your..." she stumbles over the words.

I don't supply her with the word she's looking for. Instead, I hold her gaze with my own as I answer her evenly. "Because I haven't taken a mortal life in over a century."

Her eyes go almost comically wide. "You haven't?" she asks me uncertainly, chewing on her bottom lip now.

I'm never one to lose control. I like to think that over the last century I've completely mastered the art of self-control, but seeing this little blond angel worrying that puffy pink lip between her teeth has me gripping the back of the chair to keep myself from hauling her into my arms again and biting that plump lip myself.

"But the Department..." she begins uncertainly.

I scowl as soon as I hear the organization on her

lips. "The Department of Paranormal Entities is a joke," I snarl.

She blinks, looking taken aback by my sudden vehemence. I can't it help it, though. The Department is a touchy subject with me. Like any government entity, they're completely corrupt, using their power for their own gain and to try to take down any who would stand in their way.

And I have nothing better to do than stand in their way.

It's suddenly crystal clear to me why Britney believes I killed her parents. The Department told her so.

She's one of their little vampire slayers, fueled by a need for revenge. The only reason I can think of that they would put her on my trail is because I keep blocking their bid to expand their reach over my people. Vampires are one of the few species still not under the Department's control. Being the oldest "living" vampire in existence, all of our kind defers to me. I wouldn't call myself a king of the vampires, though that's certainly how the Department sees me.

And any power that could rival their own, they see as dangerous. However, I'm of the old school mindset that no one entity needs to become too powerful. I've seen it all before. A monarch gains too much power until the ruler becomes a ruthless dictator.

No, there's a reason's America's checks and balances system works so well, and consider me one of the checks and balances to the Department. I won't be bowing to their demands any time soon. Someone has to keep them in line.

They're constantly hitting me up with new proposals of how everything in the entire world would be better for all species if we would all submit to their one-rule government—and many other creatures have fallen in line, but I refuse to allow my people to be controlled by the power-hungry machine that is the Department.

I've got my people relatively under control. Yes, the new changelings are often a handful, but I have a team that specializes in teaching vampires how to control their bloodlust and to drink without draining—and that if they must drain a body, to drink from the dregs of society, those that the human race would be better off without anyway.

"They're the ones who told you I killed your parents?" My nostrils flare, and I feel like I could breathe fire. I'm becoming angrier by the second. It's not just the fact that the Department lied on me. It's that they lied to her, this sweet, innocent little angel. They knew the potential danger they were placing her in, putting her on a suicide mission to kill me, the most powerful vampire in existence.

So, not only are they trying to get rid of me, but it looks like they're trying to get rid of her too, and what I want to know is why.

"Yes." She doesn't deny it, nodding her head instead.

I press my lips into a thin line before I reach for her hand and begin pulling her along with me.

"Wait!" she pulls against my hold, though she can't break it unless I choose to let her. "Where are you taking me?"

I stop just long enough to turn back to her, my eyes filled with promise. "To find out who really killed your parents."

Britney

I'm staring up into Henry's earnest eyes, and I can't deny the truth I see reflected there.

"Oh my god," I whisper as the realization dawns on me with the certainty of a ton of bricks. "You really didn't do it."

"No," he states the word firmly, holding my eyes the entire time, willing me to believe him.

"Then why did...?" I begin. None of it makes any sense.

Henry interrupts me, already able to tell where my thoughts are going. "That's exactly what we're going to find out," he says decisively before he begins leading me by the hand again.

I go with him willingly this time. I have no clue where he's taking me, yet somehow, I instinctually trust him now. It's crazy. I know I was just willing to kill him not more than ten minutes ago and now even though he's a vampire—and the most powerful one in the world at that—I'm letting him lead me wherever he wishes without even knowing where we're going first.

I'm either in shock or incredibly foolish, or maybe a bit of both.

I stare up at the back of his head, my head spinning with questions, as he pulls me along down many corridors. I should probably be paying more attention to which way he's taking me so that I can make a quick escape if I need to, but I'm beyond that now. We've made so many twists and turns there's no way I'll ever find my way out of here without either luck or Henry to lead the way.

He said he hasn't killed a mortal in over a

century. Does that mean he's killed some immortals? Maybe even some of his own kind?

"Henry?" I speak his name as a question. I have so many questions. I don't even know where to begin.

He halts in his tracks and goes completely still when I say his name. My face flushes when he turns his head back and looks at me with those golden eyes blazing down at me intensely.

It's the first time I've said his name, and the effect it has on him is profound. I feel my breath catch in my throat, and I fight the urge to speak it again just to keep his eyes blazing down at me like this.

I can't fully describe the feminine rush of power that flows through me at his reaction to me just speaking his name. How can just my voice have such an effect on this powerful vampire? It's a heady feeling.

He moves forward, his movements calculated, as he raises his hand up to gently cup my cheek. My heart is beating a mile a minute in my chest as I stare up at him, unable to breathe or think or do anything but just gaze into those golden eyes that are staring down at me with more emotion than I would have ever thought a vampire capable of. Want, desire, longing, sadness, and something else, something that I can't quite pinpoint but that has more humanity than I've seen in many men throughout my twenty-one years.

"Say it again," he orders me softly, and I already know what he wants me to say again, so I don't play dumb.

I swallow before I speak his name again, barely more than a whisper. "Henry."

I feel the shudder that goes through him where his hand is connected to my cheek, and the fact that just my voice saying his name can affect him like so has me feeling all sorts of things I can't identify.

"We're going to see my seer," he finally tells me before dropping his hand from my cheek.

My cheek immediately feels cold without his touch. Whoever said that vampires are cold to the touch were never in the presence of one like Henry.

His touch is like fire and ice all at once, burning me while chilling me simultaneously.

"Seer?" I question when I finally get my wits back about me enough to do so.

He gives me a faint half smile that's just as devastating as his full smile—if not more so. "You will see, little one. Make no mistake of that."

A shiver passes through me at the way he calls me "little one."

I shake my head to try to clear the fog that he somehow cast over me. I have to keep my senses here. Even if Henry didn't kill my parents, he's still a vampire, I remind myself, and while he might be as handsome as sin, I have to remember that.

CHAPTER 3

Henry

Britney cocks her head to the side and looks up at me curiously at my cryptic statement. I don't elaborate further. My words certainly do have a double meaning, though. She will see soon enough because one thing I know about Glenda is that she sees the past, present, and future, and she's never failed to make any and all three known.

While my primary reason for bringing Britney to my seer is to find out what the Department is really up to, I'm also burning to know if Glenda is going to see what every instinct in my body is already telling me—that Britney is fated to be mine.

"Almost there, little one," I reassure her as we

turn down the last corridor leading to where my seer lives.

I realize that not every vampire has their own personal seer. In fact, most vampires don't get along with those of Glenda's ilk, but we struck up a deal many years ago. I can recognize the benefits of having one with her talents in my midst.

"Here we are," I tell Britney as we finally reach Glenda's door. I give a perfunctory knock.

Glenda opens the door almost immediately, looking completely unsurprised to see us there. She no doubt already knew we were coming. That's her way.

I glance over at Britney and see her eyes widen when she takes in my seer. Contrary to what many people believe seers to look like, Glenda is far from an old hag. On the contrary, she's a redheaded vixen who oozes sensuality from every pore of her body.

"Henry," she purrs up at me like she always does. I feel Britney stiffen beside me and have to fight back a smug smirk. Is my little one jealous? Selfish being that I am, it pleases me to no end to think that she might be jealous and territorial of me already.

Yet another sign that she might really be my mate.

I merely nod down at Glenda respectfully.

While the seer has made it no secret that she would gladly take me to bed if I desired it, I've never succumbed to her charms. *Her type of experienced charm isn't what I crave anyway*, I can't help thinking as I glance over at Britney and her shining, youthful innocence.

Linda's eyes follow my gaze, and she smiles knowingly. A flicker of hope takes flight in my chest. Has she already seen that Britney is meant to be mine, or is that knowing look just because she can sense that I want the little human?

It could honestly be either coming from Glenda, although I hope it's the former rather than the latter.

"Who is this pretty little morsel?" Glenda asks, her eyes trained on Britney.

Britney apparently misinterprets the way Glenda calls her a morsel because she takes a step back, bumping into my chest. I place a hand on her hip to steady her and feel a slight tremble go through her at my touch. Sparks fly through my own body like a match on kerosene.

I feel it too, little one.

Before I can answer Glenda, she answers her own question in a blatant display of her skill. "Britney Cavill, vampire slayer for the Department of Paranormal Entities." Glenda's painted red lips turn up into a slight sneer when she speaks the Department's name. Yeah, she doesn't fancy them very much either. That's one thing we have in common and another reason why I chose her to work with.

"Yes," Britney answers evenly while straightening her back and stepping away from me.

"Henry said you might be able to help us."

I look on in amusement as Britney attempts to take charge of this entire thing. Such a fearless little thing, my human, and she looks completely adorable trying to be all brave and in charge. Glenda raises a humorous eyebrow at her before she looks up at me, obviously sharing my sentiments.

I try to keep my face impassive as I meet Glenda's gaze, though I suspect I can't keep the pride off my visage.

"Right this way then, dears." Glenda steps back and lets us into her space. Whereas her appearance might not be that of a traditional seer, her furnishings certainly are. She has sheer curtains adorned with little bead fringes hanging up everywhere as well as several orbs on stands and other little mystical-looking trinkets scattered about.

"I see your efforts to kill Henry have failed,"

Glenda calls back over her shoulder as she leads us over to her little intimate round table.

I hold the seat open for Britney and then push her in whenever she's seated. I allow my hand the lightest brush against her shoulder and hear her sharp intake of breath, though she doesn't look at me or make any comment on the motion.

My own chest tightens at that small, forbidden contact. There's no way Britney's not my fated mate—not with the way my body reacts to every glance and touch from her, but it'll still feel good to hear Glenda confirm it and to see the look on Britney's face when she hears it.

Britney doesn't answer Glenda. Instead, her lips press into a thin line as if the woman is challenging her vampire slaying skills—which Glenda might be —but it's a good thing Britney didn't succeed in her quest to kill me because she would have killed the wrong person. I didn't murder her parents and I know she wants to hold the guilty party accountable.

"So, what do we do now?" Britney asks when we're all seated around the table.

Glenda shushes her by holding up a finger as she begins to gaze deeply into the ball on her table. I have to fight from rolling my eyes. Glenda is doing this all for show purely for Britney's benefit because

I know damn well she doesn't get her visions from that ball. Anything Glenda sees she sees within her mind.

But I'm not going to deprive my old seer of her kicks. She never gets to read for anyone anymore since I took her off the market and use her solely for my purposes. And I haven't even been by for any of her advice in a good while.

"Somebody murdered your parents, but it wasn't Henry," Glenda speaks thoughtfully, and I know this part isn't an act. She's truly seeing everything now.

Britney leans forward. Her eyes flick to me—with a flash of relief?—at the confirmation that I'm indeed not the one who took her parents from her.

"The Department has told you it was a vampire who killed your parents, but it wasn't a vampire." Glenda's brows furrow, and Britney sits up straighter at this, her own brow furrowing.

"But their throats..." Britney begins," they were..."

"Completely torn out," Glenda finishes for her as she continues to gaze into her ball. She glances up at Britney and clucks at her as if she should know better—and, honestly, she should.

"That's not the style of most vampires. If a

vampire had killed your parents, there would likely not have been a drop of blood wasted."

Britney blinks, and I see her digesting that information. It indeed makes too much sense because it's true. My kind wouldn't have been so messy as to waste blood. She'd have been more likely to stumble upon perfectly clean, pale corpses had it been a vampire who murdered her parents.

I watch as the realization that the people she trusted lied to her dawns on her pretty face. Her cheeks flush, and her eyes begin to turn hard and angry. I remember what it felt like to have those heated, angry eyes on me, and while it was a bit thrilling, at least now she has that anger directed toward the right people.

"Cut to the chase, Glenda," I growl at my seer, my patience with her theatrics starting to wane in the face of Britney's obvious distress. "Who really killed Britney's parents?"

Glenda finally looks up from her crystal ball, dropping all pretense, and her face looks troubled as she glances between Britney and me.

"It was the Department," she states ominously. "They did it."

Britney

My world feels like it's crashing in all around me as everything I've believed is proved false in a moment.

The department killed my parents. It wasn't a vampire after all. So, all this time, my life's mission of hunting vampires was all for nothing.

I glance over to Henry in horror. What if all this time I've been killing innocent creatures?

Well, vampires aren't entirely innocent, but I've been killing them thinking that they were monsters who had stolen my parents' life.

Yet, it wasn't them. I look back over at the seer. Could she be lying?

No. The pity and worry in her gaze let me know that she's not. Besides, what would she have to gain from lying? No, one look into the woman's green eyes, and I can tell she's telling the truth.

"Why would they deceive this child like this, Henry?" the seer asks while casting a concerned glance my way.

"She might be their little vampire slayer, but they had to have known she was no match for me," Henry voices thoughtfully.

I glare at him, but even I have to admit the

truth in his statement—however begrudgingly. I'm no match for him.

"It's almost as if they wanted to put her in danger and have her killed," Glenda surmises.

I feel a shiver of fear run up my spine as that realization crashes over me.

The Department must have wanted me dead. Otherwise, they wouldn't have sent me on a futile mission to kill him. All this time they told me that they safeguarded the name of my parents' murderer to keep me safe. Why would they all of a sudden give it to me?

I should have known something was up, especially when they gave me the name of the most powerful vampire in the world.

Glenda's eyes take on a faraway look, though she's not gazing into the crystal ball this time. She's staring off into space, and when her eyes finally refocus, they do a curious dance back and forth between Henry and me.

"It all makes perfect sense to me now," she remarks in wonder. "I can see why you feel the way you do," she's speaking to Henry.

I stare at the pair of them in confusion. Her words are admittedly making no sense to me, though they seem to make sense to Henry. His eyes are burning with a golden light as he asks her, "Is it fated?"

Glenda nods at him before she glances back at me. "But Britney, you're not what you..."

Her words are cut off by a booming explosion. The entire floor rocks, and I see the panic in Glenda's eyes before she looks up at Henry fearfully.

"It's them. I'm so sorry, Henry. I didn't see them coming. I was too busy with you two."

"That's okay," Henry tells her as he leaps into action, rushing to my side to gather me up into his arms.

But I'm not having any of his male chauvinism. I've gone too long without answers. "Put me down!" I thrash in his hold. "I'm not what, Glenda?" I ask her hurriedly, begging her to finish her sentence.

"There's no time," Henry shakes his head as another boom rocks through the floor. His feet sway with the vibrations as his arms form a steel band around me, refusing to let me go.

"Take her someplace safe, Henry!" Glenda barks as she stands and turns toward her door. "I'll hold them off for as long as I can, but it's imperative you get out of here!"

Henry nods in understanding, but I want to scream. I was so close to getting more answers! But now Glenda's ominous statement plays at the forefront of my mind. The question is burning at me. What am I not?

I could kill Henry for keeping me from finding out the answer. I don't get the chance to protest further, though, because suddenly there's a pulling, whirlwind sensation around us, and I find myself clinging tighter to him now rather than pushing away. It's like we're swept up in a vortex, and then suddenly all is still again.

I peek open my eyes and gasp when I see that we're in something that looks like a cave underground. Only a few candles are flickering in the space of wherever we are, and I don't even have the courage to ask.

I still when my eyes light on a coffin, and I realize we're in a crypt. I glance up at Henry and one look at his face tells me the answer. It's *his* crypt.

"Put me down," I hiss at him, angry all over again that he cheated me out of my answers.

He does so wordlessly, though he doesn't release his hold on my waist as he sets me on my feet.

I try to take a step back, but Henry refuses to release me, holding me still.

"Henry, let me go," I scowl up at him with every bit of loathing I can muster, but he's smiling down at me, his eyes glowing golden in the darkness.

He moves his head down so that his mouth is right near my ear when he states, "I'm never going to let you go again, little one." Damn him. His voice is low and seductive, and it sends a shiver running through me.

"You heard Glenda. It's fated," he goes on, his voice full of promise.

I shake my head, my heart pounding within my chest at his words as I stare up at him. "What are you talking about? What's fated?"

"Us," he answers simply.

I raise an eyebrow and let out a nervous laugh as I push at his chest. It does no good, of course. He doesn't budge and neither do I.

"Henry, there is no us. You're a vampire." He frowns down at me then, and I see a bit of irritation flash in his eyes.

"I may be a vampire, but you are my mate." He squares his jaw suddenly, the sudden hunger lighting his eyes making my throat go dry.

"What?" I let out an incredulous laugh. My heart begins to hammer in my chest even harder as I pick up on what he means. "That's not possible," I whisper, "I'm a human."

Yes, I've heard the stories about vampires and their fated mates. Who hasn't? But it's only ever between two vampires—not a vampire and a human.

"Glenda must have gotten something wrong," I insist.

The look of smug assurance on Henry's face makes me swallow. "Glenda is never wrong, little one. Her visions are spot on. She said we're fated, so that proves what I already know deep in my bones."

Henry's face begins looming closer toward mine, and I already know what's on his mind. I can read the intent in his eyes. His eyes are staring at my lips, and I panic, scared that if he ever gets his lips on me, I won't have the fortitude to say no.

I push on his chest frantically now, and he finally pulls back and releases me.

"What's wrong, Britney?" His voice is dark and caressing as he speaks, his eyes pinned on me. "You know you can't fight fate," he points out.

His mouth moves close to my ear again as he says huskily, "Make no mistake, little one. You'll succumb to me before the night is out. I promise you that. You can't fight this seduction."

I scowl up at him as I cross my arms over my chest, desperately looking for any way to distract him—and to calm the flush creeping up my neck and the frenzied beating of my heart.

"Forget all this nonsense about fate for a moment." I push away from him. "Don't you think we have bigger problems to deal with right now? Like the fact that we're hiding out from the Department and why they want me and you dead." Yes, that's way more important than Henry and his libido.

Henry shrugs like it's just another day at the office for him. "I already know why they want me dead. I won't bring my kind under their rule."

His face takes on a troubled look, and he frowns. "However, what I don't understand is why they want *you* dead. What have you done to piss them off, little one?"

"Nothing!" I immediately sputter. "I've been nothing but the model employee, completing all my assignments on time—in fact, usually ahead of my scheduled deadline. I'm professional and do everything by the book. I can't think of any reason why they would want me offed. It makes no sense."

I think back frantically, trying to think of anyone that I could have pissed off, but nothing's ringing a bell. I'm not lying when I tell Henry that I was the model employee. I was and that's why this betrayal stings a lot harder. Because I know I legitimately haven't done anything to deserve this.

Again, I wonder, "Are you sure Glenda's right?"

Henry flashes me a look of irritation as he snaps, "I told you. Glenda is always right. That's why she's in my employ."

"Well, we've got to go back and figure out what's going on," I insist. "You don't really expect me to hide out here in a cave while all hell breaks loose and the Department is looking for us, do you?" I push past Henry and begin trying to find my way out of this crypt. "We need to be adults about this and confront them."

Henry puffs out a humorless laugh, "Oh, you millennials and your new way of thinking. You always think everything can be resolved with words and adult actions."

He takes a step toward me, and I step back. "I don't think you understand the kind of people you're dealing with, Britney. The department is ruthless. They don't care about you. And when they want you dead, they'll stop at nothing to achieve their aims. You can't expect to just sit down and talk this out with these people. What they've done marks an act of war, and there's no coming back from that."

Henry takes another step until he's towering directly over me, his golden eyes blazing down into mine. "And there is no way in hell I'm going to put my mate back in danger."

I glare back up at him. "I'm not your mate," I grit out slowly.

I see a vein throb in his temple as his jaw clenches at my words. I don't care if I'm pissing him off. I don't have time for his alpha male claims.

I turn on my heel and start stalking away from him. I don't know how the hell to get out of here, but I'm sure going to try to find out. Anything beats standing in this decrepit cave arguing with this insane vampire.

"Where do you think you're going?" I hear him growl from behind me.

"I'm not going to just sit here and debate with you. I'm going to do something about all this." I retort back at him without even turning around to look at him.

Henry is in front of me in a flash. I blink and stumble back. I forgot how quickly vampires could move. Probably because Henry hasn't been exercising those kinds of powers in my presence much.

"You're not going anywhere, Britney." His voice is filled with a threat, and I can't ignore the challenge.

I cross my arms over my chest and lift my chin up at him defiantly. Nobody tells me what to do. "Oh yes, I am. I'm getting out of here with or without you."

Henry lets out a dark chuckle before I'm suddenly gathered in his arms again. It happens quick as a blink—so quickly that I don't even register it until he's holding me against his chest.

My mouth falls open, "Put me down!" I scream as I begin to kick my legs and fists in the air like a child throwing a temper tantrum.

"Britney, stop!" He commands, but I'm beyond listening.

I'm panicked and frantic. My world has been completely turned upside down in the span of one evening. I go to a masquerade ball to kill the vampire who I just found out murdered my parents. But then I find out that he didn't in fact murder my parents—that it wasn't a vampire at all who murdered my parents. That it was the Department and that for some reason they're out to get me too now.

Top all of that off with the fact that I'm more attracted to this vampire than I've ever been any other man in my entire life, and now he's telling me that we're fated mates, and I'm terrified of how my body will betray me if he presses his lips against mine.

Yeah, it's a lot for a girl to take in, so I think I'm entitled to a mini meltdown right now.

"Britney!" Henry's voice cracks over me again—

like a whip this time—but that only makes me struggle even harder. I feel my heart rate ticking up in my chest until I feel like I'm about to explode.

Oh god, I'm fixing to have a panic attack. I can feel it. I used to have them as a child after my parents died. My eyes are wide and wild, I know, as I look up at Henry, silently begging for what I can't put into words. *Help me*.

CHAPTER 4

Henry

I see the sudden panic in Brittany's eyes. She's not just fighting me out of stubbornness anymore. No, this is something different. A deep-seated fear inside her. I see the silent cry for help in her desperate eyes as they latch onto mine as if I'm her lifeline.

I move on instinct. I don't know what power of the universe is telling me what to do, but I follow it without thinking.

I crash my lips down to hers, finally, finally tasting those sweet, puffy pink lips. This isn't because of lust, though. This is the kiss of a male seeking to ease the suffering of his mate.

I kiss her deeply, stroking my tongue soothingly in and out of her mouth.

She instantly quiets beneath me, going lax and pliant in my arms, melting up into me.

And while this kiss didn't begin with lust at the forefront of my mind, it quickly takes over when I register just how honey sweet her lips are. Every cell in my dead body surges to vibrant, pulsing life as I kiss her.

This is more than a kiss, though. It's a spiritual rebirthing. I feel like I'm a Phoenix being reborn from the ashes when Britney's tentative tongue moves against mine, kissing me back. A surge of victory crashes through my chest, and my arms tighten about her possessively.

All I can think is more and more and more. I need to taste her *more*.

I carry her over to the wingback chair in the corner of my cavern and settle her in my lap so that she's straddling me.

I fist my hands in the silky tresses of her golden waves and angle her head up. Even with her sitting in my lap, her head still doesn't come quite up to my own height, and I'd be lying if I said a part of me don't thrill at the fact that she's so tiny against me. Something about it causes every protective instinct within me to surge to hot, pulsing life.

She's mine and I'll kill anyone who tries to take her from me. I feel my fangs pushing against my gum line, begging to descend.

I pull back from her just long enough to fight back the urge to let them descend. I refuse to drink her blood right now. That's not what this is about.

She's breathing heavily against me, her breath coming out in little pants, fanning my lips with her sweetness.

She shakes her head dazedly as she blinks up at me. "What is this, Henry? What is this feeling? I've never..." she trails off.

"I know," I agree with her, dropping my forehead against hers. I've never felt like this before either.

I take in a deep breath before I tell her, "It's because we're fated, Britney."

I tilt her chin up to look at me, willing her eyes to meet mine and understand what I'm telling her.

She looks up at me and bites her lips uncertainly. I groan when I see the puffy pink flesh give way under her perfectly white teeth.

"I don't understand any of this," she whispers. "It doesn't make any sense. Everything I thought made sense is suddenly just the opposite. What's happening to me?" She looks up at me, and she looks so endearingly lost. My chest squeezes.

I hold my hand against the back of her neck as I look into her eyes and reassure her. "You don't have to worry about anything ever again. I'm going to take care of everything. I'm going to take care of you."

She opens her mouth, and I can already anticipate the feminist bullshit that's about to pass her lips.

"That's not me being a chauvinistic pig either. I can assure you, Britney, I'm not trying to take away your independence or control you. It's just that I come from a time when men protected what was theirs. And make no mistake of it." I whisper right against her ear now. I feel the shiver pass through her when my lips softly skate across her ear. "You are mine, Britney. There's no changing that fact. I knew it from the first moment I saw you across my dance floor. You can fight this seduction as much as you want to, but in the end, you will succumb to me," I promise her.

Her breath hitches as her beautiful blue eyes stare up at me.

"I..." She begins to speak, but she never gets the chance to finish her thought because suddenly there's a rip in the air as bright light flashes forward.

I'm standing in an instant and pushing Britney

down into the seat behind me, shielding her with my body.

Mortimer, the mage over the entire Department of Paranormal Entities, is suddenly standing behind Glenda with a knife pressed against her throat.

"I'm so sorry, Henry. I'm so sorry. I didn't tell him anything, I swear," Glenda babbles.

"But I read her mind," Mortimer replies dryly as he smirks at me. That is one of the unfortunate skills the mages have. They can read the minds of anyone. Well, *almost* anyone. They can't read a vampire's mind, which is part of why Mortimer has been so adamant about me turning my people under his rule. We're the one species he can't control, and it's killing him.

"What do you want, Mortimer?" I ask him, my voice like ice. How dare he invade my private crypt like this? This is a new level of disrespect—even from him.

"Heard you've got my best vampire slayer in your clutches, and I came to save her," Mortimer replies while attempting to peek around my body that's currently shielding Britney from his gaze.

I move to keep him from seeing her, but of course, Britney has a mind of her own and steps out from behind me.

"Liar," she hisses at him.

I see the slight surprise on Mortimer's face at her ire. No doubt he's not used to her questioning him or addressing him in such anger.

"Thirteen years you've lied to me." Her voice is shaking with rage.

I hold my arm out to block her from walking any closer to him. I don't trust him as far as I can throw him, and she might be angry, but there's no way I'm going to let my mate advance on the man—especially knowing what he's capable of.

"Britney," he croons her name like a doting father calling out to a prodigal child. He releases Glenda and immediately snaps his fingers. I watch as my seer's body drops to the floor.

She's not dead, probably just temporarily knocked out by whatever charm he cast over her.

"Who really killed my parents?" Britney demands to know. "I know it wasn't Henry. Why did you tell me it was?"

Mortimer's eyes narrow as he glances between Britney and me. "Has the vampire seduced you already?" he sneers.

Neither Britney nor I answer. Britney just stares at him with her pretty little arms folded over her chest, while I glare at him with a look that could kill.

I don't know if it's because Mortimer believes he's lost his vampire slayer for good, but his eyes take on a slightly desperate look as he pleads with Britney. "Britney, my child, you were always like a daughter to me. You know I stepped up and treated you like one of my own after your parents passed. Listen," he speaks to her now like he's sharing a deep secret with her. "I don't care what fate says. You cannot succumb to this vampire."

Britney blinks, and then asks slowly, "What do you mean what fate says?" Her eyes flick over to me, and I see the moment realization dawns on her.

"It's true then," she sounds stunned. "I'm his fated mate."

Mortimer scoffs. "Your dad was my best friend, Britney. Collum was a good guy. Just because your mother had that affair with Angus doesn't mean that you should be cursed to a fate such as this."

Britney shakes her head, her curls bouncing softly with the movement. "What are you talking about?" She asks the question slowly as she tries to process it all, but I've already processed it. I know every vampire ever in existence, and I only know of one Angus.

It all suddenly clicks in my mind as I see what happened.

"Angus was a vampire hailing from the twelfth century," I speak for Mortimer.

I level the mage in question with a look. "Are you telling me that Britney's mother had an affair with Angus?"

Mortimer's eyes flick over to Brittany with unveiled disgust.

"Oh, I see," I say as I take a step toward Mortimer. "She not only had an affair with Angus, but she had a child with him as well."

I hear Brittany gasp behind me as she starts to connect the dots herself.

"Are you telling me my dad wasn't my real dad?" she asks, her voice shaky and shocked.

"He was your father in every way that counted," Mortimer grumbles, "even against his better judgment. I told him back then that he should have made your mother abort the fetus before anything terrible came of this, but he would hear nothing of it. For some reason he loved you like you were his own." Mortimer looks her up and down like he finds her wanting, and I feel every muscle in my body tighten in defense of her. "Even though you're the spawn of a dirty, bloodsucking vampire," he spits.

"But then, that means..." Brittany speaks slowly, glancing over at me. She gasps again before she finally sees what all this means. "I have vampire blood in me," she whispers.

"Exactly," Mortimer's eyes are now dark and evil. "And all we need is another vampire on this earth."

Mortimer shrugs and moves his staff from one hand to the other. "So, unfortunately, I had to kill my best friend and his wife."

"What took you so long?" she asks. "I was eight years old when they died. Why wait?"

Mortimer scowls. "They stayed pretty well hidden. I think they knew I would come after them and their abomination."

Britney turns confused eyes back to Mortimer. "But if you hate me so much and never wanted me to be born, why did you let me live as long as you did? Why not kill me after you killed my parents?"

Mortimer actually smiles then, a sick, twisted smile. "I saw the potential in your little heartbroken eyes. That burning need for revenge. I realized I could put it to good use."

He shrugs now. "It was easy to convince you that vampires had killed your parents and to turn you into the best vampire slayer I've ever had to date."

He looks at Brittany with something akin to a

sick pride in his eyes. "I will miss you, you know. I suppose I did come to care for you in my own way."

As for Brittany, she looks like she's about to be sick.

"What changed?" I ask for her. "Why are you suddenly wanting to kill her now?"

Mortimer's mouth curls up in disgust. "When I heard the prophecy that she's fated to be your mate, I knew I couldn't have that."

That's when another piece of the puzzle clicks into place. It's not just that she's any vampire's mate, it's that she's *my* mate. I'm already the most powerful vampire in the world, but Mortimer isn't stupid. He knows that once I find my mate, I'll become a thousand times more powerful than I already am. Any hope he's ever had of defeating me would be truly out the window then.

"You really are pathetic, you know that, Mortimer," I scoff at him. "You're so blinded by your lust for power that you can't see straight. I would have never challenged you. I don't want to rule the entire world like you do. I want you to leave me and my kind alone, but ruling over all the other creatures isn't enough for you. You want the entire world."

"I'm tired of fighting you on this, vampire," Mortimer spits at me as he raises his staff high above his head. The red stone on the top of it is glowing, and I don't know what he has planned, but I'm sure it can't be anything good.

"We're going to end this today," he pronounces.

"You've got that right," I agree with him as I square off to face him, finally allowing my fangs to descend, though this time it's not in desire but out of necessity to use them as a weapon. I don't fear death, but my primary concern right now is protecting my mate.

I'm trying to decide when best to launch myself at Mortimer and tear his throat out like he did Britney's parents when the glowing red ball of his staff suddenly shoots out a stream of red light. I don't know what it is, but it's aimed right at me, and I brace myself for the impact.

I would normally dodge to the side, but I'm afraid Britney is behind me, and I don't want it to hit her instead. Whereas I can probably take the hit, it would likely demolish a mere human.

"No!" she suddenly shouts, and then I see her tiny form flinging itself in front of me with her arms held wide as if to shield me.

"Britney!" I bellow in a panic, furious that she's jumping in the way of harm even if it is to save me. Stupid, stupid girl! God, doesn't she realize she has humanity in her? She might have a little bit of vampire in her, but she's not as resilient to magic as I am.

I reach to grab her, but my hands are pushed back by blinding white light that suddenly surrounds her. It's pulsing with heat and so bright that I can't even bear to look at it.

It takes me a moment to realize that the pulsing light is emanating *from* her.

I suddenly hear a whooshing sound and look over to see Mortimer being flung back against the wall by the stream of white light.

No sooner does his head make a sickening crunch against the back of the wall and his body falls to the floor does the light disappear from around Britney.

"Britney, no!" I roar.

Mortimer's red ball of light is still traveling through the air. She doesn't have time to dodge it. It smashes directly into her chest, and she goes sailing back.

I catch her before she slams against the wall, taking the impact of her body against my chest.

We slump down onto the ground, me cradling her in my arms.

Her head lolls to the side, and fear grips me. I run my hands over her, frantically calling her name, "Britney! Britney, my love!"

I can't remember the last time I cried—certainly not since I've been a vampire, yet I feel wetness streaming down my cheeks now.

Britney's eyes flutter open weakly. "Henry," she says my name so softly, "I'm so sorry for everything." I see a sheen of tears glimmering in her own eyes, and my chest tightens painfully.

"No you don't!" My voice comes out choked as I slap lightly at her cheeks, trying to keep her eyes open. "Don't you dare, Britney! Don't you fucking dare say goodbye to me. You're going to be okay, little one."

I hear shuffling behind me and glance back to see Glenda sitting up and staring at us with tears streaming down her cheeks.

She looks between Britney and me before she nods down at my fallen angel.

"You know what to do, Henry." She encourages me.

I swallow and glance back down at Brittany, noting the weak pulse in her throat.

She's completely passed out now and not lucid at all.

"But I can't ask for her consent," I shake my head, tortured by indecision. "What if she doesn't want this?"

I look up at Glenda, seeking direction, not even

trying to hide the worry from my eyes or my voice. She already knows what Britney means to me.

"It was always going to be this way," she tells me gently. "It's fated. Now do what you must." She nods down at Brittany.

"You'll lose her if you don't," she reminds me gently when I still hesitate.

I can feel the life draining from Britney's weakened body as we speak, and I realize that Glenda is indeed right. I don't have any choice. I let her die a human death, or I activate the vampiress within her by biting her neck.

I stroke her hair back from her face, my soul knotting at the thought of never seeing her sapphire blue eyes peering up at me again.

I'm faced with an impossible choice, and the decision weighs heavily on me as I hold Britney's broken body in my arms, my soul torn in two.

What must I do?

CHAPTER 5

Henry

When faced with the choice of losing her forever or keeping her and having her be angry with me for all eternity, there's no contest. I'll take her anger over nothing any day.

Her neck is already stretched out in front of me like an offering, and I feel my fangs descend once again.

I lift her in my arms and hold her closer to me. This is not how I wanted our first bite to be.

My throat feels tight as I lick the tender flesh of her neck before I hover my lips over her skin. I press a tender kiss there, silently asking her to forgive me before I bite down and pierce her flesh with my incisors.

I groan at the perfect first taste of my mate's blood. My cock immediately swells with desire at her sweetness. She's like honey and roses and lilies and lilacs and everything sweet all rolled into one. Light yet decadent, the taste of her blood on my tongue is like nothing I've ever tasted before.

She gasps, her body arching up against me as I feel the life beginning to return to her with my bite. Since she already has vampire blood in her, there's no transformation for her to undergo. All she needed was the bite of her mate to activate her inner vampiress.

I have to force myself to stop drinking from her so I don't weaken her too much. Even without us consummating our bond yet, we are now officially mated. All it takes for vampires to mate is one bite. The cock really has nothing to do with the mating process. Of course, that part of my body is raging at me to make our union complete even in that way.

I ignore it for now, though, and pull back from her, watching as color begins to bloom in her cheeks again.

She's just as beautiful as before, yet somehow even more so in her immortality, and to think she could have died a human had I not activated the immortal blood within her.

I don't even have to lick her neck to close the wounds. The power of her own blood is already healing her.

The swollen appendage between my legs gives a jerk as I realize that now that we're mated, we'll be able to feed from one another. No longer will I have to find random people to feed from. I have my very own mate to drink from, and after what I just tasted, she's the only person I'll ever want to drink from ever again.

And I'll make damn sure I'm the only person she ever drinks from. She'll never have to taste anyone else's blood. In fact, I'll kill anyone who dares even offer it to her.

I thought I was obsessive and possessive over her before. It's nothing compared to the way I feel now. Knowing that my bite has pierced her skin has cemented something inside me. I'll never be able to let her go now even if I wanted to.

"Henry" her sapphire blue eyes blink up at me as she looks at me more lucidly than she ever has.

"You saved me," she whispers, her voice full of wonder.

I stroke her cheek tenderly, my throat tightening again when I realize how close I came to losing her. "You saved me first, my love," I whisper, my voice choking with emotion. I want to scold her for being so careless, but I can't find the words to speak. And I'm just so relieved that she doesn't seem to resent me for my choice.

"Henry," she repeats my name, and I look down into her eyes. They've taken on a half-crazed look, and she bites her lip. I smirk to myself. I know exactly what she's feeling. When vampires are newly mated, their lust is nearly out of control. Her little cunt is throbbing and aching with need, desiring to be filled by me.

She's so ready for it I can practically smell her, and my cock swells to even greater proportions.

I'm more than happy to assuage her need, but that doesn't mean I can't have a little bit of fun with her first.

"Yes, my love?" I ask her innocently. "What's wrong?"

She lets out a little whimpering sound and looks up at me with wide, pleading eyes. "Please," she begs me.

I furrow my brow as if I'm confused. "Please what? How can I help you, little one, if you don't tell me what it is you need?"

She makes a frustrated sound in the back of her throat before she finally grabs my collar and pulls me down so that my lips are hovering just over hers.

"Kiss me," she demands before she crashes her lips up onto mine.

All the desire that I've been tamping down surges forth like a freight train.

Our lips fight for dominance. I know don't know whose desire is stronger now, and I don't care. All I care about is coupling with my mate.

When Brittany tears her mouth away from mine and kisses her way over to my throat, I groan, my body shivering with the pleasure of her soft lips against my heated skin.

And when I feel her sharp teeth pierce my own skin, my eyes roll back in my head, and I nearly spill my seed in my pants.

I let out a shout as I cradle her head against my neck and succumb to the delicious feeling of her feeding from me.

I thought I was seducing her, but I was wrong, for she's definitely the seductress in this scenario.

Britney

The taste of Henry's blood on my tongue floods my senses with euphoria.

Something that I would have cringed about just a few minutes ago is making me almost dizzy with pleasure.

And I totally don't care. I can't stop this feeling flooding through me. I desire this man—this monster—like I've never desired any other, but the feeling is made suddenly way more intense with his blood flowing down my throat. I literally feel like I'll die without his touch.

And that's ironic, isn't it? Because technically, I'm dead, right? If I'm a vampire, I'm dead. Yet, I've never felt more alive.

Henry lets out a deep, guttural groan that sounds like it's being ripped from the depths of his soul, and god help me if that doesn't do something to me.

I answer with a whimpering little moan of my own. It's all I can manage in between drinking up the sweet blood that's coursing down my throat as I clutch onto his shoulders and press my body up against him, gyrating my hips instinctively up against the hardness that I feel between his legs.

He hisses in a breath and gently puts a hand against my neck to push me away from him. "Easy, there, little one. Not too much at first," he cautions me.

I let out a sound of protest as he pushes me away from the sweet nectar of his neck.

"I want more," I tell him unashamedly as I look up at the two little holes that are already healing on his neck.

I lift my hand to feel the side of my own neck where he bit me and find that there are no holes there either.

I must have healed myself likewise.

"How is this possible?" I ask him in wonder as I search his eyes.

He licks his lips as he settles himself over me with an elbow on each side of my head. "You already had vampire blood in you from your father," he explains to me. "All you needed to activate it was the bite of your mate."

He gives me a cocky grin at that last statement.

"So, I'm completely a vampire now?" I ask just to be sure.

He nods his head.

"So, that means I'll have to drink blood from now on?"

He frowns before he states definitely, "Only mine. You'll never drink blood from anyone else. You'll never be a murderer, so don't worry about that either. I'll teach you everything you need to know about self-control." His lips quirk up into a heart-stopping grin, "And I'll enjoy every moment of your instruction."

My face flushes at the innuendo in his words, and then my eyes settle on his lips. I feel a tingle in my own lips. I want to have his lips pressed against mine again, and I'm tired of fighting this seduction. I want him. I need him inside me more than I've ever needed anything in my entire life.

He seems to read the intent in my eyes because when I lift my hands up to him in supplication, he comes down to me willingly, pressing his lips insistently against mine. He immediately parts my lips with his tongue.

"Dammit, Britney, but you're perfect. Perfect, perfect mate," he whispers into my mouth as he strokes my hair back from my face.

I lean into his touch, practically purring as I lift my hips and rub myself against him again, half-crazed with need.

He hisses in another breath. "My God, you're going to be the death of me woman."

I cock my head to the side. "Aren't we already technically dead, though?"

He cracks a grin, his fangs gleaming down at me. "On the contrary, my love," he whispers against my lips as he begins pushing up my dress. His hand skates over my calves and up my legs before they skirt over my thighs. My breath hitches the closer he gets to my aching core. "I've never felt more alive," he nearly growls. Each touch of his fingers sends tingles throughout my body, and I can feel his hardness pressing against my leg.

He stills when his fingers reach the apex of my thighs. I feel him test my wetness, and his light touch sends tingles straight through me. I let out a groan and arch up into him, throwing my arms around his neck.

"Please, Henry! Please!" I beg him.

"God, you're so wet," he murmurs as he begins to kiss his way down my neck and over my shoulders. He trails his lips over my collarbone and the exposed swell of my breast.

"I don't know if I can go slow, my love." His voice is ragged as he yanks down the top of my dress to reveal the aching rosebuds of my breasts. He takes one into his mouth, suckling it, and I arch up into him, pressing my breasts up into his mouth, offering myself to him. The sensation is like there's a live wire connecting my nipple to that little bundle of nerves in between my legs because I feel the sensation register down there as much as it does on my breast.

God, I don't ever want him to stop. Everywhere his fingers touch, everywhere his mouth lands, feels so decadently good. If you could die of pleasure, I'd be dead now.

"I don't want you to go slow," I tell him honestly. I feel like I'm going to combust at any minute. The need I have for him is an all-consuming thing. It demands reparation. *Now.* "I just want you to take me, have me completely. Now!" My voices comes out in a high whine at the urgency I feel.

Henry swears, and then I feel him hastening to unbuckle his breeches. He pulls them down just enough to free his massive erection. I barely get a glimpse of the swollen purple head bobbing in the air between us before I feel it prodding at the hole between my thighs.

I clamp my hands onto Henry's arms, anticipation lighting my every nerve ending.

"Mine!" Henry grits out between clenched teeth as he pushes up into me hard, claiming me in one swift motion.

I scream, letting out a keening sound as my hymen gives way to the invasion of his swollen flesh.

He swears again as he settles deep within my slick channel and holds himself still, his hard rod pulsing within me in time to the beating of our hearts.

"Britney, my love," he stutters out as if it's taking everything within him to remain still. I can feel the tautness of his muscles beneath my hands, and the muscles in his neck are bulging too. His jaw is hard, and his eyes are dark and wild with lust when he gazes down at me with such possession it takes my breath away.

I feel his pain. I feel like I'm going to die if we don't move, so I take the initiative and begin rocking my hips against him.

"Christ Almighty," he grits out, sweat breaking out on his forehead, before he takes over and begins slamming his hips against me over and over again.

I feel his long rod stroking in and out of me, creating this delicious friction that has every nerve ending snapping and crackling to life.

I wrap my arms and legs as far around him as I can get them and hold on tight as he rides me. He ruts into me in a tango as old as time itself.

And it's glorious.

I've never felt more complete than I do in this moment. This isn't just sex. This is something spiritual. We're worshiping each other, ascending into something greater than we are on our own.

I feel this intense pressure building within me right behind my belly button. Then Henry's length and girth somehow gets impossibly longer and thicker within me.

"Henry!" I call out his name in half question, half begging. I don't really know.

"Yes, my love. I'm right there with you," he encourages me. "Let go. Give it to me."

He ruts into me one more time, hard and deep. Something bursts deep within me. I scream while he roars, and then our mouths are falling on each other's necks as we both bite down simultaneously.

The taste of his blood hitting my tongue at the same time I feel mine coursing into his mouth along with the spasming and convulsing of our bodies together sends me into a mindless, endless orgasm unlike anything I could have ever imagined. Granted, I've never had an orgasm before, but something tells me that this is more than any simple orgasm. This is the ultimate pleasure of being completely fated to your mate, and I'm wondering now why I fought it so hard.

We eventually lick each other's necks gently as we come down from our euphoria and float back to earth.

I open my eyes to see Henry's golden eyes

glowing down at me with the look of a satisfied tiger.

I smile up at him, and he smiles back at me lazily before he rolls onto his side and pulls me into his arms.

He strokes my hair back from my face and lifts my chin up to softly press his lips against mine once again.

He kisses me tenderly this time, languidly taking my lips in his own, and I can feel the love pouring from his mouth into mine.

"I told you so, little one," he tells me smugly.

I look up at him quizzically with a raised eyebrow.

His mouth tugs into a wide grin, and his eyes twinkle down at me mischievously as he elaborates, "I told you you'd succumb to me by the end of this night."

I laugh and slap at his chest playfully before burrowing my head against him.

I feel his laugh rumble throughout his big chest, and I've never felt more at home than I do in this moment.

"I love you, Britney," his husky voice whispers before I feel him drop a kiss on the top of my head.

My heart swells. "I love you too, Henry," I

confess the words and feel them settle in my soul where they burn like a roaring fire.

Where they'll burn for centuries to come.

82

THE END

Want more books by Kenzie Skye?

Visit Kenzie Skye's website at www. authorkenzieskye.com.